What's Forever?

written by Jennifer Goodhart Gonzalez

illustrated by Unada

Library of Congress Catalog Card No. 85-62949
© 1986. The STANDARD PUBLISHING Company, Cincinnati, Ohio
Division of STANDEX INTERNATIONAL Corporation. Printed in U.S.A.

Sometimes when Mother is talking to Aunt Phyllis on the telephone, Dad says he thinks those two could talk forever.

And when Dad sits around watching football games, Mother says she thinks football season will last forever.

Some days when I'm sitting in class listening to Mrs. Malone talk about our math assignment, I look out the window and wish I could be playing ball with Jason and Jesse. On those days I feel like school will never end.

Last week I went to Jason's birthday party. When I asked Dad how long it would be before my birthday, he said six months. That seems like forever to me.

I practice on the piano every evening before dinner. It seems like I'm forever playing scales, but Mother says that isn't so.

I love going to Grandma's and Grandpa's, but they live far away. When we drive to their house, the trip seems like it takes forever.

But those things don't really last forever.
It just seems that they do. In fact, there
isn't much that lasts forever.

Lots of things aren't around for long—
like Mother's chocolate chip cookies.

Or the paper airplanes Dad and I make.

Or ice cubes on a sunny day.

Or the puddles in the gutter after a heavy rain.

Or the snow forts we build in the winter.

Last year Mother and I planted petunias.
They looked beautiful all summer, but
when the cold weather came, they died.

I asked Dad about the maple tree beside my bedroom window. He said it has been there as long as he can remember, and it will probably still be there for a long time. But someday it will die, too.

Buildings and statues last a long time.

So do some roads and bridges.

But they don't last forever.

I wanted Josie, my pet turtle, to last forever, but she got sick last week and died.

Even people die. Most of us will live for a very long time. But someday we will die. That's part of God's plan, Mother says.

So what lasts forever? Dad says only one thing lasts forever – Heaven.

When we die and join our friends and family in Heaven, we will be there forever. That's what people mean when they talk about eternal life – it goes on and on and on and on without ending.

It's all part of God's plan for us.